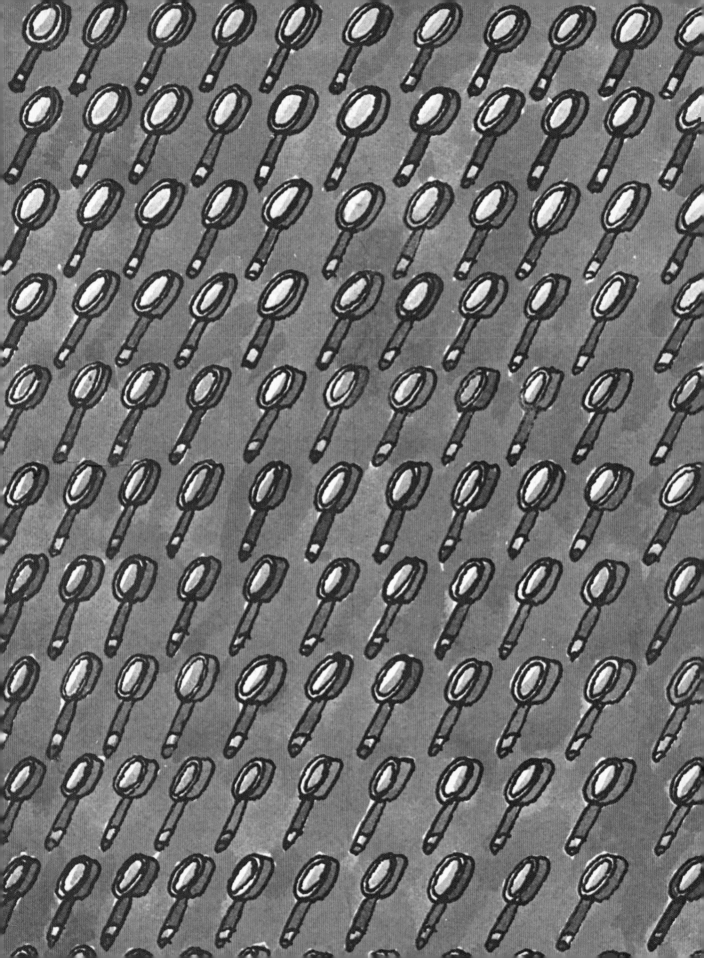

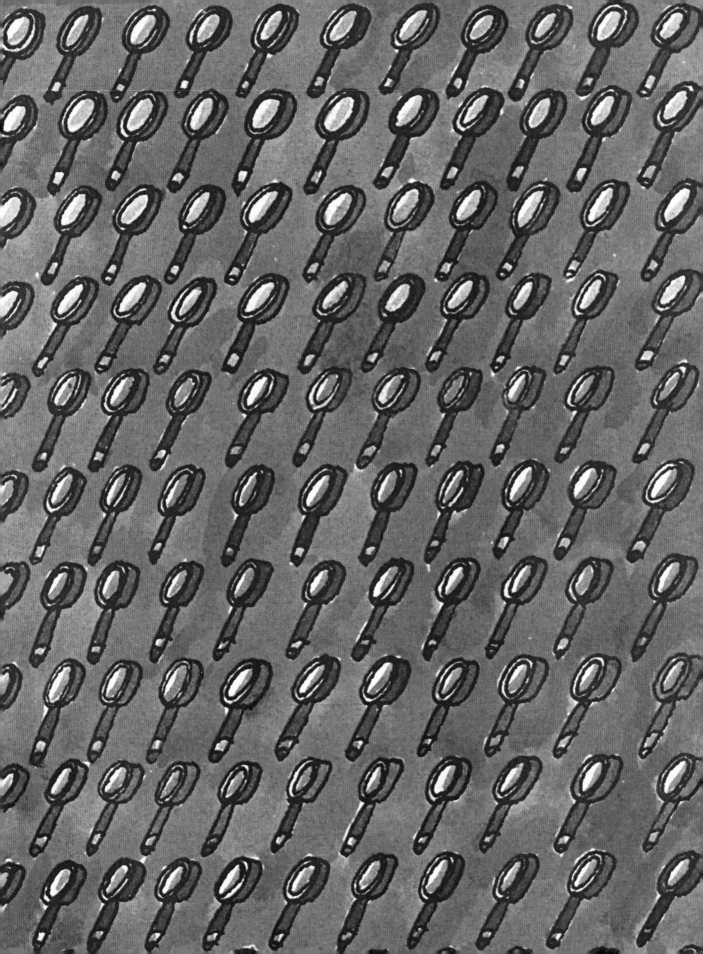

FOR PIET

and all the children in Iowa,
and now for Emma and Aidan

—R. Q.

ALADDIN

An imprint of Simon & Schuster Children's Publishing Division

1230 Avenue of the Americas, New York, New York 10020

First Aladdin paperback edition January 2021

Copyright © 1986 by Robert Quackenbush

ALADDIN and related logo are registered trademarks of Simon & Schuster, Inc.

For information about special discounts for bulk purchases, please contact

Simon & Schuster Special Sales at 1-866-506-1949 or business@simonandschuster.com.

The Simon & Schuster Speakers Bureau can bring authors to your live event.

For more information or to book an event contact the Simon & Schuster Speakers Bureau

at 1-866-248-3049 or visit our website at www.simonspeakers.com.

Book designed by Tiara Iandiorio

The illustrations for this book were rendered in watercolor, pen, and ink.

The text of this book was set in Neutraface Slab Text.

Manufactured in China 1020 SCP

10 9 8 7 6 5 4 3 2 1

Library of Congress Control Number 2018941548

ISBN 978-1-5344-1521-8 (hc)

ISBN 978-1-5344-1522-5 (pbk)

ISBN 978-1-5344-1523-2 (eBook)

SHERLOCK CHICK'S

First Case

Robert Quackenbush

ALADDIN NEW YORK LONDON TORONTO SYDNEY NEW DELHI

**HERLOCK CHICK'S** first case began on the day he was born.

At once, Emma Hen and Harvey Rooster knew that he was special.

With that, his proud parents named him Sherlock.

His first words were, "Are you in need of a detective?"

"Yes, we are," said Emma Hen. "You've come just in time!"

She pointed to an empty feed bin in the chicken yard. "Someone has taken our corn!"

Sherlock Chick went with his parents
to the feed bin. "Who do you think took
the corn?" he asked.

"We don't know," said his parents.

"I will look for clues," said Sherlock
Chick. He walked around the feed bin.
"Aha!" he said.

What did he see?

He saw a trail of corn.

It was leading out of the yard.

"I will follow this trail," said Sherlock Chick. "I will find your corn and bring it back."

"That's our boy!" said his parents.

Sherlock Chick followed the trail of corn.

Suddenly he stopped.

What did he see?

He saw a horse.

"Do you like corn?" asked Sherlock Chick politely.

"No," said the horse. "Grass is my favorite thing to eat."

The horse had not taken the corn.
So Sherlock Chick went on his way,
following the trail. He stopped again.

What did he see?

He saw a goat.

"Do you like corn?" asked Sherlock Chick politely.

"It's all right," said the goat. "But eating the paper off cans is much more fun."

The goat had not taken the corn.

So Sherlock Chick went on his way, following the trail.

He stopped again.

What did he see?

He saw a pig.

"Do you always eat your corn on the cob?" asked Sherlock Chick politely.

"Yes," said the pig. "The cobs are my favorite part."

The pig had not taken the corn.

So Sherlock Chick went on his way,
following the trail.

He stopped again.

What did he see?

He saw a scarecrow.

"Do you like corn?" asked Sherlock Chick politely.

"I never touch it," answered the scarecrow. "I'm here to chase crows away. They like corn a lot."

"Aha!" said Sherlock Chick. "I think I know who took the corn from the chicken yard."

He hurried on his way.

The trail of corn led to an old barn and stopped there.

Sherlock Chick peeked through a crack in the barn door.

What did he see?

He saw three crows.

They were pecking away at a pile of corn.

It was the corn from the chicken yard!

Sherlock Chick had a plan.

He ran and got the horse, the goat, the pig, and the scarecrow to help.

They went with him to the barn.

The horse put the scarecrow next to the barn.

The goat knocked down the barn door.

The pig ran through the barn squealing, "Oink! Oink!" as loud as he could.

The crows flew out of the barn and right into the scarecrow.

"Awk! Awk! Awk!" they cried.

They were so scared that they flew away and never came back.

Sherlock Chick and his friends brought the corn back to the chicken yard.

"This case is closed," said Sherlock.

Emma Hen and Harvey Rooster were so happy to have the corn back that they had a big party and invited everyone.

And that is the end of
Sherlock Chick's first case.

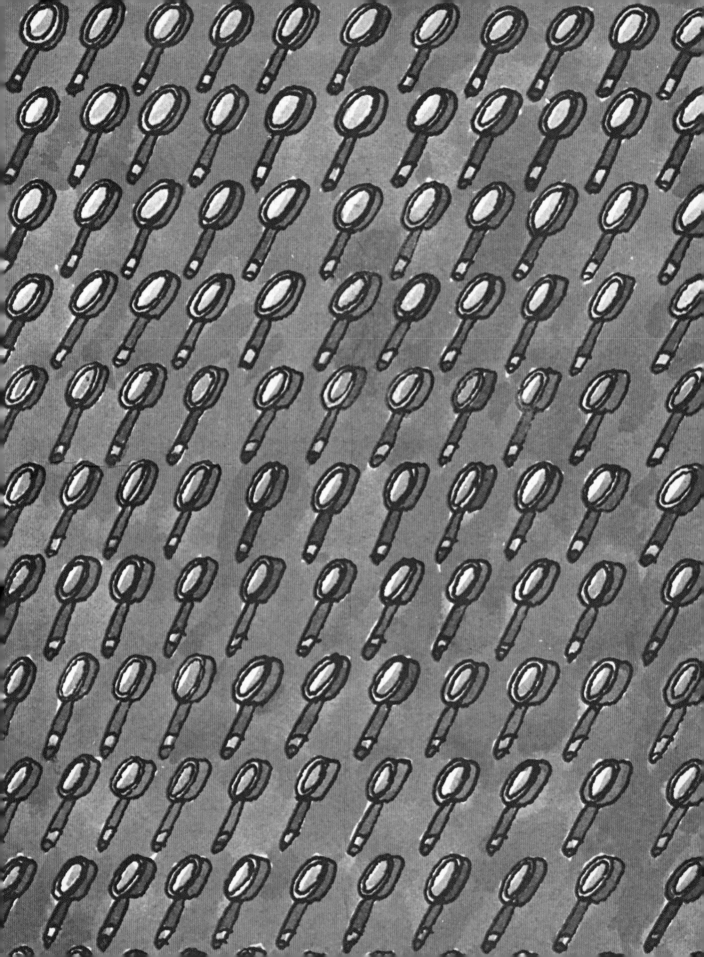

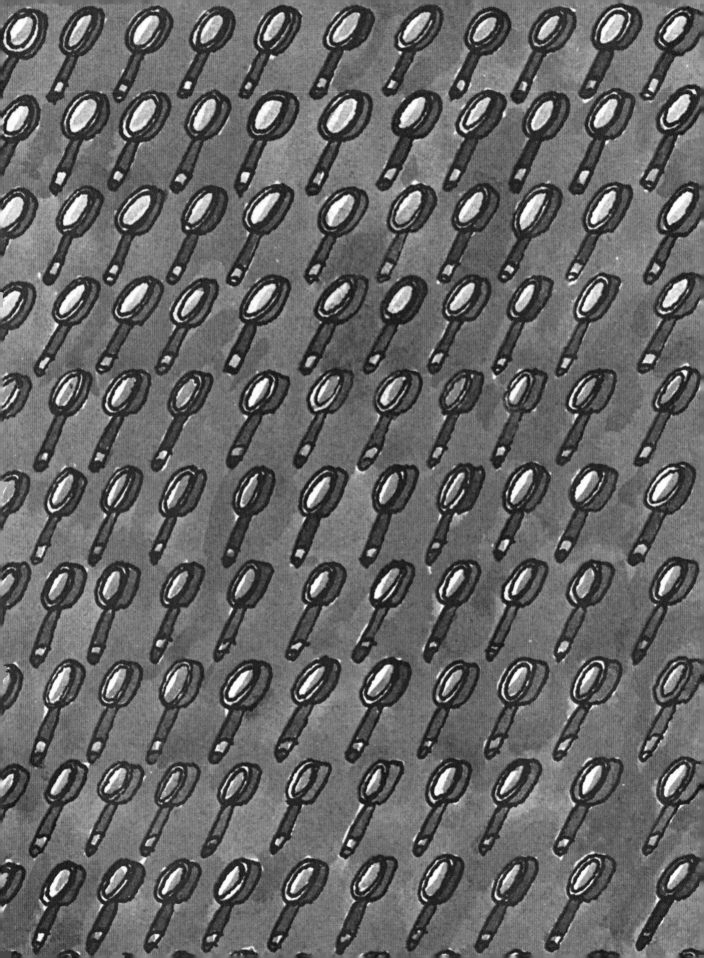